I'm glad God made me—JUST RIGHT!

TROPICAL SATYRID BUTTERFLY/PHOTOGRAPH BY JAMES L. CASTNER

_____ _____
name   date

God Made Everything— Just Right!

A BOOK ABOUT CREATION

Karen Bigler
Illustrated by Bartholomew

Chariot Books™
David C. Cook Publishing Co.

Chariot Books™ is an imprint of David C. Cook Publishing Co.
David C. Cook Publishing Co., Elgin, Illinois 60120
David C. Cook Publishing Co., Weston, Ontario
GOD MADE EVERYTHING—JUST RIGHT!
First Printing, 1990. Printed in the United States of America
94 93 92 91 90 5 4 3 2 1
ISBN 1-55513-278-2 LC 89-60319

God made the sky.
He made it . . . JUST RIGHT!
He made the moon,
    the clouds,
    the stars,
    the sun,
    the planets.
God made the sky.
He made it . . . JUST RIGHT!

God made the land.
He made it . . . JUST RIGHT!
He made the grass,
    the rocks,
    the hills,
    the mountains,
    the deserts.
God made the land.
He made it . . . JUST RIGHT!

God made the water.
He made it . . . JUST RIGHT!
He made the oceans,
 the rivers,
 the lakes,
 the brooks,
 the rain.
God made the water.
He made it . . . JUST RIGHT!

God made the fish.
He made them . . . JUST RIGHT!
He made the salmon,
    the tuna,
    the cod,
    the trout,
    the shark.
God made the fish.
He made them . . . JUST RIGHT!

God made the animals.
He made them . . . JUST RIGHT!
He made the cow,
    the horse,
    the dog,
    the cat,
    the lamb.
God made the animals.
He made them . . . JUST RIGHT!

God made the birds.
He made them . . . JUST RIGHT!
He made the sparrow,
    the robin,
    the sea gull,
    the dove,
    the eagle.
God made the birds.
He made them . . . JUST RIGHT!

God made the flowers.
He made them . . . JUST RIGHT!
He made the lily,
    the daisy,
    the rose,
    the tulip,
    the pansy.
God made the flowers.
He made them . . . JUST RIGHT!

God made the trees.
He made them . . . JUST RIGHT!
He made the fir tree,
    the fig tree,
    the pine tree,
    the palm tree,
    the oak tree.
God made the trees.
He made them . . . JUST RIGHT!

God made you.
He made you . . . JUST RIGHT!
God made your eyes,
    your nose,
    your mouth,
    your arms,
    your legs.
God made you.
He made you . . . JUST RIGHT!

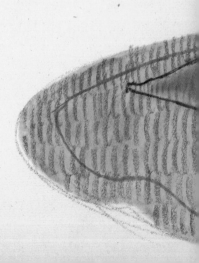

God made everything!
He made the sky,
   the land,
   the water,
   the fish,
   the animals,
   the birds,
   the flowers,
   the trees.
And God made you.
God made everything . . . JUST RIGHT!